A Frog in My Throat

A Frog in My Throat

FRIEDA WISHINSKY

Illustrated by
Louise-Andrée Laliberté

ORCA BOOK PUBLISHERS

Library and Archives Canada Cataloguing in Publication

Wishinsky, Frieda
A frog in my throat / written by Frieda Wishinsky ; illustrated by
Louise-Andrée Laliberté.

(Orca echoes)
ISBN 978-1-55143-632-6
I. Laliberté, Louise-Andrée II. Title. III. Series.

PS8595.I834F76 2008   jC813'.54   C2007-907391-3

First published in the United States, 2008
Library of Congress Control Number: 2007942399

Summary: When Jake starts spending time with his cousin,
Kate feels hurt and seeks new friends to play with.

Orca Book Publishers gratefully acknowledges the support for its publishing programs
provided by the following agencies: the Government of Canada through the Book
Publishing Industry Development Program and the Canada Council for the Arts, and the
Province of British Columbia through the BC Arts Council
and the Book Publishing Tax Credit.

Typesetting by Teresa Bubela
Cover artwork and interior illustrations by Louise-Andrée Laliberté
Illustrator photo by Marc Riverin

ORCA BOOK PUBLISHERS
PO Box 5626, STN. B
VICTORIA, BC CANADA
V8R 6S4

ORCA BOOK PUBLISHERS
PO Box 468
CUSTER, WA USA
98240-0468

www.orcabook.com
Printed and bound in Canada.
11 10 09 08 • 4 3 2 1

With thanks to Maggie de Vries and Maureen Colgan.

Chapter One
DUMB MOVIE

"Want to see *Revenge of the Ghost* tomorrow?" Kate asked her best friend Jake.

"Sure," said Jake.

Kate and Jake loved *Revenge of the Ghost*. They'd seen it three times already, but they still loved watching it.

They loved to scream when the ghost appeared in the captain's room.

They loved to screech, "I'm back," when the ghost screeched, "I'm back."

They loved to howl when the ghost took off his head and carried it down the hall like a hat.

"See you tomorrow at two," said Kate.

"I'll bring potato chips," said Jake. Jake always brought potato chips.

The next day, Kate filled a bowl with popcorn and a plate with chocolate chip cookies. She'd helped her mom bake the cookies that morning. The house still smelled of chocolate. It was the best smell in the world.

At two fifteen, Kate looked out the window. She didn't see Jake, but she wasn't worried.

Jake was always late.

Last week his excuse was that he didn't have any clean underwear. The week before he said the zipper on his pants broke. Kate smiled. What crazy excuse would he have today?

Kate opened the door and peeked out. There was Jake! He was walking down the street with his mom and a tall boy. The tall boy had red hair and freckles just like Jake.

Who was he?

"Sorry we're late," said Jake. "But my cousin Lionel just came over. He's moving to our neighborhood next week."

"How nice," said Kate's mom.

"Can he watch the movie too?" asked Jake.

"Of course," said Kate's mom.

Lionel plunked down on the couch in the den. Jake flopped down beside him. Kate slipped the movie into the player. Then she curled up in the big chair.

The movie began.

"I've seen this movie before," said Lionel. "It's dumb."

"I know," said Jake, "but it's funny."

The ghost floated into the captain's room.

Kate screamed.

"Are you scared of the ghost?" Lionel asked her. "He doesn't even look like a ghost."

"Yeah," said Jake, "he looks fake."

Kate glared at Jake. "He looks real to me," she said.

The ghost screeched, "I'm back," but Kate didn't screech. She felt silly screeching alone.

Jake didn't look like he was going to screech. He didn't look like he was even watching the movie.

He was too busy talking to Lionel.

"This movie is really dumb," said Lionel. "Want to play video games?"

"We don't have any," said Kate.

"You're kidding," said Lionel.

"We have some at my house," said Jake. "We can play them later."

"Great," said Lionel.

The ghost took his head off and carried it in his arm.

"This is the stupidest movie in the world," said Lionel.

Jake nodded. "I know," he said. "It's really dumb."

How could Jake say that? thought Kate. He loved *Revenge of the Ghost*.

Lionel picked up a handful of potato chips and crunched them in his mouth. Then he made a face like a clown. Jake laughed.

"Shhh," said Kate, but Lionel crunched some more potato chips. He made a face like a baboon.

Jake laughed and laughed.

Kate glared at Lionel, but Lionel kept crunching.

"Cut it out!" said Kate.

"Sorry," said Lionel. "I forgot you were watching the movie."

"I can't anymore," said Kate. "It's over."

"Hey, Jake," said Lionel. "Want to go to your house and play video games?"

"Sure," said Jake. "I'll call my mom."

Soon Jake and Lionel left.

Kate ran to her room and flung herself on her bed.

"What's the matter?" asked her mom.

"I hate Lionel," said Kate. "He said the movie was dumb, and he crunched potato chips and made stupid faces."

"Maybe he's too old for the movie," said Kate's mom. "He's two years older than you and Jake."

"He doesn't act older. He acts like a baby, but Jake thinks he's funny."

"Jake is just trying to be nice to his cousin," said Kate's mom.

"But why isn't Jake nice to me?"

"Don't worry. Jake is still your friend," said her mom. "And remember, Lionel will be in grade four. He won't be in your class."

It was true. Jake was in her class, not Lionel. Lionel would just be at her school.

But he'd be there every day.

Chapter Two
PARTNERS

Kate slid into her seat before the first bell.

Jake wasn't in his seat yet.

The bell rang.

Their teacher, Mr. Bolin, hurried into class.

"Before I take attendance," he said, "I have a wonderful surprise. We're going to the chocolate factory in two weeks."

"Yahoo!" shouted all the kids.

"We'll learn how cocoa is grown and how chocolate is made," explained Mr. Bolin. "And the factory promised to give each of us free chocolate samples."

"Hurrah!" shouted the kids.

Kate couldn't wait. She loved free samples, especially free chocolate samples, and she knew Jake did too.

Kate pictured the trip with Jake.

It would be so much fun sitting on the bus together.

It would be so much fun being partners.

It would be so much fun eating free samples.

But where was Jake? He was always late but not this late. Was he sick?

Just then, Jake dashed into class.

He handed Mr. Bolin a note. Mr. Bolin read the note and smiled.

"I'm glad your goldfish didn't die this time," said Mr. Bolin.

Everyone laughed. Jake was famous for his crazy excuses.

"It's nice that you were able to show your cousin around school this morning," said Mr. Bolin. "When is he starting school?"

"Next Monday."

"Good! Just in time for our trip. His grade four class will be going to the chocolate factory with our class. We may even take the same bus."

"Neat!" said Jake.

Kate gulped. What if Jake wanted to sit near Lionel on the bus? What if he wanted to be partners with Lionel on the trip?

If she didn't sit next to Jake, who could she sit with? She hardly ever played with anyone else. And the only kids who didn't have regular partners in her class were Leo, Brad and the new girl, Patty.

She couldn't sit near them.

Leo shot spitballs into her hair. Brad had a drippy nose. And Patty was so shy that she hardly ever said a word.

All through math and reading, Kate worried about the trip.

The recess bell rang.

"Race you to the swings," said Jake.

"One. Two. Three. Run!" called Kate.

Kate ran as fast as she could. So did Jake.

They reached the swings at the same time.

"Tie," said Jake. He hopped on a swing.

Kate hopped on the next swing.

"Isn't it great that Lionel will go on the trip with us?" Jake asked.

Kate didn't say anything. She began to pump. Her ponytail bobbed up and down as she flew.

"So what do you think?" asked Jake.

"About what?" asked Kate.

"About Lionel, of course."

"Well…," muttered Kate.

"Isn't he the funniest kid you ever met?" asked Jake.

"No," said Kate.

"Who's funnier than Lionel?"

"I don't know," said Kate.

"Lionel knows a thousand jokes. I hope he's on our bus to the chocolate factory."

But Kate hoped he wasn't.

Chapter Three
BACK TOGETHER

On Tuesday, Jake didn't mention Lionel once.

Jake didn't mention Lionel as they played catch at first recess. He didn't mention Lionel as they climbed rocks at the back of the yard at second recess.

By the time they walked home together after school, Kate had almost forgotten about Lionel.

"I hope they give us milk-chocolate samples at the chocolate factory," Kate told Jake. "Milk chocolate is my favorite."

"I hope they give us milk-chocolate-with-caramel samples," said Jake. "I love caramel."

"Maybe they'll try out new chocolate bars on us," said Kate.

"Yeah. Like chocolate with spinach?"

"Or broccoli," said Kate.

"Or chocolate with sardines!" said Jake.

"How about mashed-up hot dog bits?" suggested Kate.

Soon Jake and Kate were laughing so hard they couldn't talk.

It felt like old times.

On Friday after school, Jake came over to Kate's house.

"Let's play in your walk-in closet," suggested Jake.

They loved playing in the closet. It was big and dark and spooky.

Sometimes it became a jungle, and they hunted lions.

Sometimes it became a time machine, and they went back to caveman days. Sometimes they went forward in time and became robots.

"Let's fly to Mars today," suggested Kate as she opened the closet door.

"Look out!" said Jake. "There's a green alien behind you."

Kate spun around. "Yikes!" she screamed. "His eyes look like slimeballs."

Jake grabbed Kate's arm. "There are three more aliens behind you. And they have ray guns."

Kate grabbed a wire hanger. *Pow. Pow. Pow.*

"Got 'em!" she said.

"Look. They've melted into green mush," said Jake, pointing to a rolled-up green sweater on the floor.

"But here come three blue aliens."

"Don't worry. They're carrying signs," said Jake. "Their signs say *WE COME IN PEACE*."

"Yeah, right. I don't believe them. It's a trap," said Kate.

"Listen," said Jake. "What's that noise?"

"I don't hear anything," said Kate.

"Someone is saying my name," said Jake, "for real."

Kate and Jake listened. Sure enough, someone was calling Jake's name. It sounded far away, but the sound was coming closer and closer.

Kate grabbed Jake's hand. Jake's hand was sweaty.

"Jake! Jake!" The voice was louder and louder. "Are you in there?"

"Oh," said Kate. "It's just my mother." Kate opened the closet door.

"Oh, there you two are," said Kate's mom. "Your mom wants you to come home, Jake. Your cousin Lionel and his mother have just come over to your house."

"Great!" said Jake, and before Kate could say good-bye, he dashed out the door.

Kate slumped on her bed. Everything had been going so well. Everything was the way it used to be.

But now it wasn't.

Lionel was back.

Chapter Four
NOTHING TO DO

"There's nothing to do," Kate told her mom on Saturday.

"Call Jake. You usually play with him on Saturday," suggested her mom.

"He's probably busy with Lionel. Lionel's moving to our neighborhood today."

"Call anyway. Jake might not be busy all day."

Kate sighed. "Okay. I'll call, but I bet he'll be busy."

Kate dialed Jake's number.

"Hi, Kate," said Jake in his usual friendly voice.

"Do you want to come over and watch a movie?" asked Kate.

"I can't," said Jake. "I have to help Lionel move his stuff today."

"How about tomorrow?" asked Kate. "We could watch a movie and play in my closet."

"I can't," said Jake. "We're taking Lionel and his parents out for lunch. Then Lionel is showing me his new computer games. Isn't it great that Lionel lives only two blocks away from me?"

Kate wanted to scream, No, it's not great!

But she couldn't scream. She couldn't say anything. She felt like she'd just swallowed a frog and it was stuck in her throat.

"See you at school," said Jake.

Kate slammed down the phone. "I wish I hadn't called," she told her mom. "Jake is busy all weekend with Lionel. He'll probably be busy all year with Lionel. Then I'll have nobody to play with."

Kate ran to her room. She punched her pillow. She buried her head in her quilt.

"Come on, Kate," said her mom, opening the door. "Let's go to the movies."

"I don't want to go to the movies. I don't want to do anything. I'm never leaving my room."

Kate's mom sighed. "If you change your mind," she said, "let me know."

Kate's mom shut her door.

Kate crawled under her quilt. She closed her eyes, but when she did, all she could hear was Jake and Lionel laughing. All she could see was Jake and Lionel playing computer games.

Kate opened her eyes.

She jumped out of bed. She grabbed her new book, *Mystery on Planet Zebra.*

Jake said it was good. Jake said that when she finished *Planet Zebra*, he'd give her his copy of *Mystery on Planet Ape.*

Kate slammed the book shut. Her room was full of Jake. Jake's books. The closet they played in. She even had Jake's socks in her drawer. He had left them there when they played Desert Island three weeks ago.

Jake was everywhere in her room. She had to get out or she'd really really scream.

Kate opened her door.

"Let's go to the movies, Mom," she said.

Chapter Five
LOST

For two hours, Kate forgot about Jake and Lionel. The movie was funny. The popcorn was fresh and crunchy.

When Kate and her mom returned home, Grandma May was there.

"How about a game of cards?" asked Grandma May.

Kate and Grandma May played ten games of cards. Kate won six. Grandma May won four.

Saturday passed.

Sunday was busy too.

Kate's mom baked a cake and Kate helped her.

Kate's Aunt Claire came over with her new baby and new dog. Kate played with the new dog. The new baby was too little and cranky to play.

24

Kate almost forgot about Jake and Lionel all Sunday, but at eight o'clock she remembered.

It was back to school tomorrow. School meant Jake and Lionel. School meant no one to play with at recess.

"You don't know that for sure," said Kate's mom. "Remember, Lionel is in grade four. He'll probably want to play with grade four kids."

"I hope so," said Kate.

The next morning at school, Jake missed the bell. As he slid into his seat five minutes after it rang, the kids laughed. They were waiting to hear his latest excuse.

"So," said Mr. Bolin, trying to hide a smile. "What's it this time?"

"It's my cousin Lionel's first day at school. I had to help him find his classroom."

"Didn't you show Lionel around school last Monday?"

"Yes, but Lionel forgot where to go."

The kids twittered.

"Lionel is in fourth grade, right?" said Mr. Bolin.

"Right," said Jake.

"I think he can find his classroom by himself," said Mr. Bolin. "And I hope you'll start to find your way to your classroom on time, Jake. Otherwise, you may not be able to join us at the chocolate factory next week."

Jake's face fell.

"But...But...," he sputtered.

"No buts, Jake. And no more excuses."

Jake sank down in his seat. "He really did get lost," he said under his breath.

It was "read aloud" morning. Mr. Bolin read the class a funny story. Everyone laughed, including Jake and Kate. By the time Mr. Bolin had finished and they'd talked about the story, it was recess.

Kate stood up. Jake stood up. He smiled at Kate. Kate smiled back.

They walked out of the classroom together. Jake didn't seem to be in a hurry to rush out and meet Lionel. He seemed happy to talk to Kate.

Maybe Mom was right. Maybe Lionel was playing with the kids in grade four.

Kate told Jake she liked the beginning of *Mystery on Planet Zebra*.

"Great," said Jake. "I have all ten Mystery Planet books now. You can borrow them."

"Where did you get them?" asked Kate.

"They used to be Lionel's," said Jake. "He gave them to me when I helped him organize his room. Hey, there he is," said Jake. "See you."

And with that, Jake took off.

Kate stood in the middle of the yard. All around her, kids were talking and running. They were sliding, playing catch, jumping rope and chasing each other.

Kate didn't know where to go. She didn't know what to do. She didn't know who to be with or talk to. The whole playground was full of friends playing together.

But she didn't have any friends to play with. Not anymore.

Chapter Six
GRUMPY

It was the longest, loneliest recess ever.

Kate was happy to hear the bell. She was happy to be back in class. She was happy to do math, even though math was her worst subject.

"Lionel is so funny," said Jake as he sat down beside her. "He knows more jokes than a comedian."

Kate didn't say anything. She just opened her math book and began to do question one.

"Why are you so grumpy?" asked Jake.

"I'm not grumpy," said Kate. "I have to concentrate on math."

"Oh, math," said Jake. Jake didn't like math either.

"My mother has been telling me I'd better concentrate more on it too."

Kate nodded and kept her eyes on her paper. She tried to concentrate on math. But all she could think about was that she had no one to play with at recess. And what about going home? She and Jake usually walked home together. Would Jake walk home with her or would he take off with Lionel?

As soon as the home bell rang, Jake popped out of his seat. "See you tomorrow, Kate. I have to meet Lionel in front of the school. I promised I'd help him put his baseball cards in an album. He must have a thousand!"

Jake flew out the door. Kate swallowed the lump in her throat. She put her books away and walked out of the classroom. Her mother was waiting for her.

"Hi, Kate," said her mother. "How was school?"

"Terrible," said Kate. "Jake follows Lionel around like a puppy. He doesn't want to be with me at all. It's just Lionel, Lionel, Lionel!"

"What are you going to do?" asked her mom.

"I don't know. All I know is Jake's not the only person in the world," said Kate. "There are other people I can be friends with."

"That's the spirit, Kate," said her mom. "It's good to have lots of friends."

"Tomorrow I'm going to play with Sarah and Marlee," said Kate. "They always ask me if I want cookies. And I went to both their birthday parties this year."

Kate smiled. "I feel much better now. Jake can play with Lionel all he wants."

The next day, right before the bell rang, Kate marched over to Sarah's and Marlee's desks.

"Want to play together at recess?" she asked.

"Sure," Sarah said. "Do you have any dolls?"

"Dolls?" said Kate. "No, not with me."

"That's okay," said Marlee. "You can use ours today."

"Thanks," said Kate.

Kate walked back to her desk. Dolls? She never played with dolls. Well, today she was going to start. How hard could it be?

Chapter Seven
DOLLS

"Here, Kate, this is your doll," said Marlee. "Her name is Roberta."

Kate looked at Roberta. She had long black hair, a short red dress and skinny legs.

"She looks more like a Cindy to me," said Kate.

"Her name is Roberta," said Marlee.

"Oh," said Kate.

"Now," said Sarah, "Roberta is best friends with my doll, Linda, and they are going shopping."

"And this doll is Lara," said Marlee, holding a blond doll in a short yellow dress with skinny legs. All Marlee's and Sarah's dolls had short dresses and skinny legs.

"What's Lara doing?" asked Kate.

"Lara is going shopping too, and she will bump into Roberta and Linda at the store. She doesn't know that Roberta and Linda are buying her a birthday present."

"Oh," said Kate. "Are they doing anything else except shopping?"

"After shopping they are going to have lunch," said Marlee.

"And then maybe they could go roller-skating?" suggested Kate.

"No," said Sarah, "they don't like to roller-skate."

These dolls don't like to do anything except shop and eat, thought Kate.

Roberta, Linda and Lara bought five pairs of shoes, two purses and six pairs of pants and had cream cheese-and-tuna sandwiches for lunch.

Kate tried to look interested, but it was hard. Kate hated shopping for shoes, purses or pants. She liked eating lunch, but she didn't like playing lunch.

"Want to go down the slide?" she asked Marlee and Sarah after the dolls had finished lunch.

"Not now," said Sarah. "We haven't ordered dessert."

"How about after dessert?" said Kate.

"Maybe," said Marlee, "but the dolls may be too stuffed to go down the slide."

"I don't mean the dolls," said Kate. "I mean us."

"I really don't like the slide," said Sarah. "I once bumped my knee at the bottom."

"Me neither," said Marlee. "I once got a splinter in my finger from the wood."

Kate sighed.

The bell rang. Recess was over.

"Tomorrow, let's play fashion show," said Sarah.

"Yes!" said Marlee.

Yuck, thought Kate.

Chapter Eight
A NEW FRIEND

"Did you bring your dolls today?" Sarah asked Kate the next morning before class.

"No, I only have one doll and her arm fell off," said Kate.

"Well, you can still play dolls with us, but having your own doll is better."

"I guess so," said Kate. "See you at recess."

Kate walked back to her seat. She didn't want to play dolls again. But if she didn't play with Sarah and Marlee, who could she play with?

Kate was so busy worrying, she didn't see the foot sticking into the aisle. She stepped on it.

Kate looked up. It was Patty's foot.

"Sorry," said Kate.

"It's okay," said Patty, looking up at Kate with her big green eyes. "I was reading and I forgot my foot was sticking out."

"Hey, you're reading *Mystery on Planet Zebra*. I love that book."

"Me too," said Patty, smiling shyly. "I want to read all the Mystery Planet books."

Kate was surprised. Patty didn't usually say much. She'd just moved to their school, and she was usually so quiet that you didn't know she was there.

"What chapter are you on?" asked Kate.

"Six. But I'll probably finish the book by tonight. I can't stop reading it. It's so good."

"Hey, Patty," said Kate. "Do you want to play at recess?"

"Yes," said Patty. "I have some sidewalk chalk. Do you want to draw?"

"I love making sidewalk pictures," said Kate. "Let's meet at the back of the school at recess."

Patty's round face glowed.

The bell rang. Kate slid into her seat. To her surprise, Jake was in his seat on time. He'd been on time for the last two days.

Jake was doodling. He was drawing a picture of two boys playing computer games. One boy looked tall and the other was short. Kate knew who the boys were: Jake and Lionel. But today, Kate didn't feel bad about Jake and Lionel.

Mr. Bolin walked into the classroom and told the class to write a page on "What I Want To Learn at the Chocolate Factory." As Kate wrote, she worried about what she'd say to Marlee and Sarah. How could she tell them she didn't want to play dolls?

As soon as the bell rang, Kate ran over to them. "I don't think I'm good at playing dolls," she said.

"That's okay," said Marlee, combing her short brown hair. She and Sarah gave each other relieved looks. Kate knew they were happy to play by themselves again.

"See ya," Kate said, and she raced out to the back of the school. Patty was waiting with a box of sidewalk chalk. For the rest of recess, Kate and Patty drew rockets, monsters and cats in green, blue, violet and red.

Patty was great at drawing cats. She showed Kate how to make fat cats, skinny cats and fluffy cats.

"Let's draw again tomorrow," suggested Kate.

Patty's big smile told Kate she couldn't wait.

Chapter Nine
TOO MANY PROMISES

By recess the next day, it was official.

Patty and Kate were going to be partners on the bus to the chocolate factory.

Kate and Patty bounded into class after recess.

"If I get a milk-chocolate sample," said Patty, "you can have it."

"If I get a dark-chocolate sample, you can have it," said Kate.

Kate slid into her seat beside Jake. He didn't look up from his book.

Mr. Bolin told them that their art assignment was to draw a rain forest. "Chocolate is made from cocoa beans," he explained. "And cocoa beans grow in the rain forest."

Kate drew cocoa trees in the rain forest. She drew parrots flying between the trees. She drew a parrot perched on a girl's hand. But Jake wasn't drawing. He was just staring at his paper.

"Hey, Jake," Kate asked. "Why aren't you drawing? You love to draw."

"I don't feel like it," muttered Jake. He looked sad.

"What's the matter?" Kate asked.

"Lionel," muttered Jake. "He won't play with me anymore. He says I'm a little kid, and he wants to play with big kids."

"Oh," said Kate. Jake looked so miserable that Kate almost forgot how he'd dumped her for Lionel.

"I don't care," said Jake. "Lionel's not that funny anyway. And he didn't even like *Revenge of the Ghost*—the best movie ever."

"I know," said Kate.

"I only said I didn't like it before because…well… just because," said Jake.

Kate nodded. She knew Jake had been showing off to Lionel.

"Can we play together again?" asked Jake. "I know I've been hanging around with Lionel a lot and... well...You're still my best friend, Kate. And... I'm sorry."

"Sure we can play," said Kate. It was hard to stay mad at Jake. Especially when he said he was sorry.

"Hey, that's great. And we could play pirate ship in your closet this weekend. That is, if you want to."

"Sure," said Kate.

"I'd better start drawing," said Jake, smiling his old goofy smile. Jake picked up a blue marker.

Kate smiled. Jake was happy to be friends again. And she was too.

"Are you sitting with anyone on the bus to the chocolate factory?" Jake asked as he drew a giant cocoa pod.

Oh no, thought Kate. What should she do? She had promised to sit with Patty, but then Jake wouldn't have anyone to sit with. And if she didn't sit with Patty, Patty would be all alone on the bus.

"I…I…," stammered Kate.

"Aye, aye, Kate m'mate!" said Jake, beaming.

Oh no, thought Kate. Jake thought she said "yes" in pirate talk. Now she was in real trouble.

Chapter Ten
OLD TIMES

"I can't wait to go to the chocolate factory," said Jake on the way home from school. Jake talked about how much fun they'd have on the bus ride. He talked about how much fun it would be sharing free samples.

It felt like old times, but it wasn't like old times. Now there was Patty.

What was Kate going to do?

Kate couldn't stop thinking about Jake and Patty. Everyone in the class had a partner, even spitball Leo and drippy-nose Brad. They were partners with each other. There had to be a way for Kate, Jake and Patty to be partners. But how?

On the way to school the next morning, Kate still didn't know what to do.

She slipped into her seat just before the bell rang. Jake slid into his seat a minute later.

"Let's finish those rain forest pictures," Mr. Bolin told the class. "I want to display them in the hall."

Kate drew two parrots on a tree in the rain forest. One more parrot on the branch and I'm finished, she thought. But there was no room on the branch for another parrot.

Where can I put him? she wondered.

Maybe...Yes! Suddenly Kate knew what to do about the third parrot—and what to do about her friends.

"Mr. Bolin," she said, raising her hand, "could I talk to you—privately?"

"Come on up to my desk."

Kate hurried up to Mr. Bolin's desk. She told Mr. Bolin about wanting to be partners with Patty and Jake. "If I'm partners with one person, the other person won't have anyone to sit next to," she explained. "So I have an idea."

Kate told Mr. Bolin her plan.

"I like your plan," he said. "Let's talk more at recess."

Kate zoomed back to her seat.

"What's up?" asked Jake.

"Tell you at recess."

"Okey-dokey," said Jake, finishing his rain forest picture.

As soon as the recess bell rang, Mr. Bolin asked Kate, Jake and Patty to come to his desk.

"Kate has a problem. She wants to be partners on the chocolate factory trip with both of you," Mr. Bolin told them, "but you know the two-person-per-seat rule."

Kate glanced at Jake and Patty. They didn't look happy.

"But Kate came up with a great plan," said Mr. Bolin. "Do you want to tell them about it, Kate?"

"It's a way we can all be partners," said Kate, "and Mr. Bolin can have a partner too. On the bus to the factory, Mr. Bolin and Jake can be partners, and I'll be partners with Patty. On the way back, we'll switch. Mr. Bolin and Patty can be partners, and I'll be partners with Jake. But we'll all sit in the same row so we'll all be together. And Mr. Bolin promised to tell us jokes on the bus."

"What about at the chocolate factory?" asked Jake.

"There's no two-person rule there, so the three of us can all be partners together!" said Kate.

"Is that okay with you?" asked Mr. Bolin.

"Well…," said Jake. "Do you really know a lot of jokes?"

"Lots," said Mr. Bolin.

"Great. I know some too. I'll tell you on the bus."

"How about you, Patty?" asked Mr. Bolin.

"Do you want the window seat?" she asked.

"No, I like aisle seats better," said Mr. Bolin. "That way I can stretch out my legs."

Mr. Bolin had long legs.

"Good!" said Patty. "I love the window seat. I'll be your partner."

"Hurrah!" sang Kate. "This is going to be the best and most delicious trip ever!"

She felt so happy that they'd all be partners and friends, she wanted to jump up and dance.

So she did.

Louise-Andrée Laliberté has built a career as an artist, illustrator and graphic designer in both English and French. She was awarded CAPIC's Gold Prize for book illustration for *L'Homme Étoile*. She is also the illustrator of Susin Nielsen-Fernlund's *Hank and Fergus* (a Mr. Christie Silver Seal Award winner, Orca 2003) and *Mormor Moves In* (Orca 2004). She lives in Quebec with her family.

Frieda Wishinsky is an international award-winning author of many popular books for children, including *Dimples Delight*, *A Noodle up Your Nose* and *A Bee in Your Ear*, all Orca Echoes. She lives in Toronto, Ontario, with her family.